A Sherlock Holmes Alphabet

By P. James Macaluso Jr.

To the memories of EDWARD GOREY

and ARTHUR CONAN DOYLE

A is $\int$ or AGRA,

the immense treasure found.

B is for BASKERVILLE,

accursed by the hound.

C is for CHARLES,

the worst villain of all.

D is for DREBBER,

held lifeless beside a bloodstained wall.

E is for ECCLES,

befuddled by the clocks.

F is for FRANCES,

alive in a pine box.

G is for GARRIDER,
a killer so named.

H is for HUDSON,

the landlady most famed.

I is for IRENE,
who enchanted a king.

J is for JEPHRO,

who confined his offspring.

K is for KIRWAN,

silenced by a gunshot.

L is for LESTRADE,

the best of a bad lot.

M is for MYCROFT,

whom the government trusts.

N is for NAPOLEON,

the six plaster busts.

O is for OPENSHAW,

found dead in the slime.

P is for PROFESSOR,
the master of crime.

Q is for QUARTER,

the missing rugby back.

R is for ROYLOTT,

done in by snake attack.

S is for SHERLOCK,

consulting detective.

T is for **TURNER,** overly protective.

U is for URCHINS,

the irregular force.

V is for **VINCENT**,
who showed little remorse.

W is for WATSON,

the devoted colleague.

X is for XIXth,

a century of intrigue.

Y is for YARDERS,

bewildered by the truth.

Z is for ZU GRAFENSTEIN,

saved by the great sleuth.

Notes on the text

A. In *The Sign of Four*, the Agra treasure is a vast hoard of precious stones and jewels brought back to England from India by Major John Sholto. After Sholto's death, his son Bartholomew finds the stolen treasure hidden in a concealed room in the roof of the family house.

B. In *The Hound of the Baskervilles*, the evil Hugo Baskerville and later Sir Charles and Sir Henry Baskerville are haunted by a gigantic spectral hound, which apparently roams the moors near the family estate in Devon and caused the death of the former two men.

C. In 'The Adventure of Charles Augustus Milverton', the titular character is a professional blackmailer who uses a league of spies and informers to extort money from his victims. Sherlock Holmes is repulsed by Milverton and thus describes him as "the worst man in London".

D. In *A Study in Scarlet*, the body of Enoch J. Drebber is found in an unoccupied house in London. The killer, as a ploy to fool the police, scrawled in blood the word 'Rache', or revenge in German, on one of the walls of the room in which the deceased was discovered.

E. In 'The Adventure of Wisteria Lodge', John Scott Eccles does not understand how Aloysius Gracia, his host for an evening at Wisteria Lodge, looked in on him in his bedroom at nearly one o'clock in the morning, as the man was allegedly murdered before this time.

F. In 'The Disappearance of Lady Frances Carfax', Lady Frances, a lone and unwed woman, falls under the influence of a fake clergyman who takes her prisoner, pawns her valuable jewels, and then inters her, while unconscious, in a coffin along with an elderly dead woman.

G. In 'The Adventure of the Three Garridebs', John Garrideb, an alias of James Winter, uses the peculiar surname to effect an introduction to a Mr. Nathan Garrideb, who unknowingly possesses a printing press and plates to make counterfeit money in a hidden cellar of his house.

H. Mrs. Hudson, first appearing in *A Study in Scarlet*, is the landlady of 221B Baker Street, the legendary residence of Sherlock Holmes and Dr. John Watson. In 'The Adventure of the Dying Detective', Watson describes her as "long-suffering" due to Holmes's singular habits.

I. In 'A Scandal in Bohemia', Miss Irene Adler, later to become Mrs. Irene Norton, was the mistress of the hereditary King of Bohemia. She outwits Sherlock Holmes, as well as the King, when the two men seek to recover compromising letters and a photograph in her possession.

J. In 'The Adventure of the Copper Beeches', Jephro Rucastle imprisons his daughter Alice in a room in an unused wing of their house so that he and his second wife can maintain control of the inheritance his daughter was set to receive from her deceased mother when she came off age.

K. In 'The Adventure of the Reigate Squires', William Kirwan, a coachman, is murdered by his employers, Alec Cunningham and his father, as he tried to blackmail the two men after witnessing them break into a neighbor's house in order to retrieve an important legal document.

L. Inspector G. Lestrade of Scotland Yard appears in *A Study in Scarlet* and twelve other stories. In *A Study in Scarlet*, Holmes identifies Lestrade and another detective, Tobias Gregson, as "the pick of a bad lot...both quick and energetic, but conventional—shockingly so".

M. Mycroft Holmes is the corpulent and highly intelligent older brother of Sherlock, who works in some government office. In 'The Adventure of the Bruce-Partington Plans', Sherlock reveals that "Occasionally he *is* the British government [...] the most indispensable man in the country".

N. In 'The Adventure of the Six Napoleons', a thief appears to be randomly smashing busts of the French leader. Inspector Lestrade believes it to be the work of a madman, but Holmes deduces that one of the plaster statues secrets a priceless missing gem, the black pearl of the Borgias.

O. In 'The Five Orange Pips', Elias Openshaw, the uncle of Sherlock Holmes's client John Openshaw, is found "face down in a little green-scummed pool" at the foot of the garden after receiving a letter containing only five dried orange seeds and bearing the mark K.K.K.

P. Professor James Moriarty, who appears in 'The Final Problem' and *The Valley of Fear*, is Sherlock Holmes's greatest opponent. He is described by Holmes as "the Napoleon of crime... [...] He is the organiser of half that is evil and of nearly all that is undetected in this great city...".

Q. In 'The Adventure of the Missing Three-Quarter', Godfrey Staunton, the star player for the Cambridge University rugby team, disappears a few days before an important match against Oxford, to be with his secret wife, who is dying of consumption, in her final moments.

R. In 'The Adventure of the Speckled Band', Dr. Grimesby Roylott, who practiced medicine in India, murders one of his stepdaughters before her marriage and attempts to do the same to the other, only to be attacked and killed by his own venomous snake, the cryptic speckled band.

S. Sherlock Holmes of 221B Baker Street declares himself in *A Study in Scarlet* the "world's only private consulting detective". He uses his keen powers of observation and deduction to help solve complex, and often odd, cases for clients ranging from simple governesses to kings.

T. In 'The Boscombe Valley Mystery', John Turner, the overprotective father of Alice, bludgeons to death his neighbor and former conspirator in crime to prevent the marriage of his daughter to the deceased's son, James McCarthy, whom Turner deems an unworthy suitor.

U. The Irregulars, or the "Baker Street division of the detective police force", are a group of street children, or urchins, employed by Sherlock Holmes as intelligence agents. Holmes asserts "there's more work to be got out of one of those little beggars than out of a dozen of the force".

V. In 'The Red-Headed League', Vincent Spaulding is the alias of John Clay, the fourth smartest man in London. When captured by Holmes and company trying to steal gold bullion from the City branch of one of the principle London banks, Clay is quite defiant and unapologetic.

W. Dr. John H. Watson, intelligent and honourable, is Sherlock Holmes's friend, assistant, sometimes flatmate and notably biographer. Holmes refers to Watson as his "trusty comrade" and "chronicler" and even admits "I am lost without my Boswell".

X. The majority of cases investigated by Holmes and Watson occurred in the latter part of the nineteenth century during the reign of Queen Victoria, a time of significant advances in the fields of forensic science and criminology, as well as the growth of detective fiction.

Y. In addition to Inspector G. Lestrade, numerous other detectives and constables of Scotland Yard, or the Metropolitan Police Service, appear in various Sherlock Holmes stories, and nearly all of them are described by Holmes as "lacking in imagination" and "out of their depths".

Z. In 'His Last Bow', Count Von und Zu Grafenstein is the uncle of the Von Bork, whom Holmes has been feeding false information in the guise of Altamont. To reveal his true identity to the German agent the detective says: "it was I…who saved from murder…your mother's elder brother."

Other books by the author

SHERLOCK HOLMES RE-IMAGINED: The original Sherlock Holmes stories delightfully illustrated using only LEGO® minifigures and bricks. There are 13 individual books in the series, as well as a complete edition that combines the first 12 stories into a single volume.

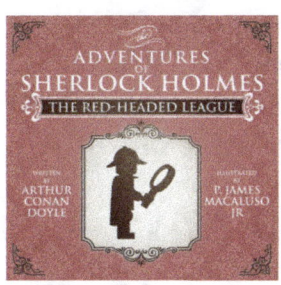  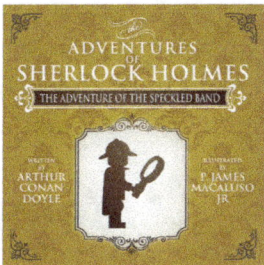

Other books by the author

THE LEGEND OF SLEEPY HOLLOW RE-IMAGINED: The original and unabridged text of Washington Irving's ghostly tale accompanied by twenty-eight charming color photographic illustrations featuring custom designed models built using only LEGO® brand minifigures and bricks.

The text of the rhyming verses in this book is typeset in ZOMBIFIED designed by CHAD SAVAGE and freely available at SINISTER VISIONS.COM.